The Battle Begins

Written by Michael Teitelbaum
Illustrated by Dreamwave Studios

Reader's Digest
Children's Books

Pleasantville, New York • Montréal, Québec • Bath, United Kingdom

TRANSFORMERS™ Flip Book Fun

On the upper right-hand corner on the opposite page, you'll see a TRANSFORMERS logo. Flip the pages and watch the logo change!

CE

Published by Reader's Digest Children's Books
Reader's Digest Road, Pleasantville, NY U.S.A. 10570-7000
and Reader's Digest Children's Publishing Limited,
The Ice House, 124-126 Walcot Street, Bath UK BA1 5BG
Text copyright © 2003 Reader's Digest Children's Publishing, Inc.
Reader's Digest Children's Books is a trademark and Reader's Digest
is a registered trademark of The Reader's Digest Association, Inc.
All material other than text, HASBRO and its logo, TRANSFORMERS, AUTOBOTS, DECEPTICONS,
MINI-CONS and all related characters are trademarks of Hasbro, and are used
with permission. © 2003 Hasbro. All rights reserved.
Manufactured in China.
10 9 8 7 6 5 4 3

Contents

Prologue

Cybertron
Four million years ago

Deep in space, in a distant galaxy, a titanic battle raged on the planet Cybertron. The population of the planet was divided in half, with each side waging cosmic war on the other. Both sides suffered many losses, and Cybertron's once-great civilization crumbled into chaos.

But it was not always this way. For many years, Cybertron was a peaceful place where freedom ruled and the quest for knowledge guided the population.

The planet Cybertron was unique in all the universe. Home to a race of intelligent, mechanical beings called Transformers, both the planet and its inhabitants were created by a powerful force known simply as the Creator.

Cybertron itself was an intelligent planet that had its own consciousness and life force. The planet could learn and grow in knowledge just as the Transformers themselves grew. In addition to their great intelligence, Transformers also had the ability to change their shape.

They could re-form themselves, changing into the likenesses of machines or vehicles. At first, this skill was used for exploration and knowledge, but it was soon applied to the waging of war.

In Cybertron's early years, the Transformers evolved into a sophisticated, flourishing society. This peaceful race of robots traveled into space, visiting other worlds. Their goal was to expand the Transformers' civilization throughout the universe, and to acquire knowledge.

After each space mission, the Transformers returned home and downloaded new information about other cultures into the consciousness of their entire race. This new knowledge was also downloaded into the consciousness of Cybertron itself.

Aiding the Transformers in all their activities was a second race of mechanical beings, called the Mini-cons. This smaller race of machines had also been fashioned by the Creator.

The Mini-cons attached themselves to the Transformers, increasing and enhancing their powers. The Mini-cons were considered helpful tools that made the lives of Transformers easier.

Over time, however, the Transformers split into two groups. The first called themselves Autobots. These robots maintained the vision of peace, liberty, and the quest for knowledge that had always been the way of life on Cybertron.

A second group emerged, calling themselves Decepticons. These Transformers craved power and domination. They viewed space travel as a way to gain control over other worlds.

The Decepticons also used the Mini-cons to increase their powers. Unlike the Autobots, though, the Decepticons treated the Mini-cons cruelly, viewing them as slaves, rather than tools.

And so, a great war broke out—the Autobots against the Decepticons. Both armies tried to dominate and control the Mini-cons, fighting for ownership of the small, but useful machines. Each side hoped to gain control over the Mini-cons, realizing that they increased the power of any Transformer who combined with them.

Both sides believed that the Mini-cons held the key to victory. The war escalated, with each side constructing massive warships that lit up the night sky over Cybertron with fiery explosions. The struggle for control of the Mini-cons almost destroyed Cybertron.

As the final battle of the First Great War between the Autobots and the Decepticons unfolded, all the Mini-cons were gathered together in a giant orbiting storage facility. This last encounter would be winner-take-all, with the Mini-cons as the grand prize.

During the battle, giant warships from both sides

collided with Cybertron's moon. The resulting impact destroyed the moon.

Jagged fragments of the moon orbited Cybertron, serving as a reminder of the destructive power of the war. Realizing that their precious planet could easily suffer the same fate as their moon, the Autobots and Decepticons called a truce. Both sides had suffered great losses in the war, and the Transformers had grown weary of constant battle and destruction.

As part of the truce, it was decided that the Mini-cons would be placed in a spaceship and launched away from Cybertron, so that they would never again be used as pawns in a terrible war. The Mini-cons' ship was equipped with a "warp gate" device which would instantly transport both the Autobots and the Decepticons to the ship if it was ever intercepted. This was done to guarantee that no other races from other worlds could get hold of the powerful little machines.

That's when something remarkable happened—something that neither side in the war had anticipated. By placing all the Mini-cons together in close quarters on the spaceship, their group intelligence grew. A spark of consciousness ignited. Soon the desire to be independent beings, free to choose their own destiny, overwhelmed the Mini-cons.

No longer would they be satisfied being tools, or

worse, slaves, for the whims of the Transformers or anyone else. The Mini-cons were actually a separate race of intelligent mechanical beings put on Cybertron by the Creator. Although they were engineered to enhance the stronger Transformers, the desire for independence was always within them.

Unaware of this development, the Transformers launched the Mini-cons' ship into space, hurling the vessel to a distant galaxy.

Back on Cybertron, the Mini-cons were eventually forgotten. Autobots and Decepticons went about rebuilding their world. Over many centuries and millennia, the existence of the Mini-cons faded into the realm of legend. Many Transformers grew to doubt that these now-mythical machines ever existed.

Eventually, war broke out again between the Autobots and Decepticons on Cybertron. Although the Mini-cons had become nothing more than an ancient myth, the horror of war was once again all too real.

Meanwhile, the Mini-cons' spaceship emerged from the warp gate into the Milky Way galaxy—and into the solar system containing the planet Earth.

But something was wrong.

The warp gate had damaged the ship's guidance mechanism. Reeling out of control, the Mini-con ship slammed into Earth's moon and broke apart. One section of the ship lay buried in the lunar dust, scattering Mini-cons all around the moon.

The rest of the ship fell to Earth where it crashed. It shattered into thousands of pieces, scattering the remaining Mini-cons around the planet. The impact left all the Mini-cons—on both the Earth and moon—unconscious. They were stranded on two worlds millions of miles from home. The section of the Mini-cons' ship that crashed on Earth ended up buried deep within a mountain. At this time on Earth, humans had just discovered fire, and were living in caves. These primitive people had no understanding of the strange objects that had fallen from the sky, or the monstrous explosions they saw coming from the mountains.

Many years passed. The Mini-cons remained buried and dormant as the Earth underwent huge changes. During this time, humans evolved, civilizations rose and fell, cities and towns were built, and major wars were fought. Airplanes were invented, followed by jets, then spaceships landing on the moon, and finally space shuttles that brought cargo to orbiting space stations.

In the year 2010, humankind was still unaware that a great power lay buried on their planet. They were also unaware that the most innocent of beings were about to awaken this awesome power and bring an age-old conflict to the planet that they called home.

Chapter 1

The Cosmo Kids

The Cosmo Scope Research Center and Interstellar Observatory was home to many families in the mountainous region of western Colorado. This facility was so large that it included a residential area, where the scientists who worked at the observatory and their families lived.

The astronomers and researchers who worked at the center were studying distant galaxies and interstellar phenomena. Their work was at the cutting edge of human knowledge about space, the stars, and the possibility of life on other planets.

The center had a school that the employees' children attended. The Cosmo Kids, as the students at the school jokingly referred to themselves, rarely traveled far from the complex. They hardly ever got to meet kids from other towns, and so they depended on each other for friendship and fun.

RIIIIIING!

The bell signaling the end of another school day echoed through the halls of the large cinder block building. Excited students ranging in age from 6 to 14 burst through the doors, free to spend the rest of the warm, early autumn afternoon as they pleased.

A 10-year-old boy with dark, curly hair came tearing down the ramp leading from the school on a skateboard. He spun to a stop, kicked his board up, and snatched it from the air with his hand.

"Hey, Rad!" he called out to a 12-year-old boy with blonde hair, who was pulling his BMX bike from a nearby bike rack. "Did you bring the equipment?"

"You bet, Carlos!" cried Rad, grabbing the handlebars of his bike, launching himself into a handstand, then landing with his feet on the pedals, while balancing the bike perfectly in one spot. His real name was Brad, but no one except his mother called him that. He preferred Rad, nicknamed for his radical moves on the bike. "I brought a flashlight and walkie-talkies."

"And I brought the fuel!" shouted an 11-year-old girl with short, straight black hair. She skidded to a stop on her scooter, pulling up beside the boys. She held out three chocolate-covered energy bars.

"Awesome, Alexis!" yelled Carlos, as the three banged their fists together in a gesture of friendship that had become their standard greeting. "Chocolate energy

bars are my favorite!"

"And, of course I brought Rover along," Alexis added, reaching around and patting her backpack. Rover was the name the three friends gave to Alexis's powerful handheld computer. The device was no bigger than a cell phone. Not only could it download wireless video e-mail, it also had a built-in Global Positioning System (GPS) tied into a satellite orbiting the Earth.

"That's cool," Rad said, as he lifted his bike up onto its back wheel, like a cowboy rearing up on his horse. "Let's move!"

The three friends sped away from the school, Rad on his bike, Carlos on his skateboard, and Alexis on her scooter. Within seconds, they had left the school grounds and were heading out of the complex.

Two 11-year-old boys on BMX bikes watched as the trio tore down the bumpy road, kicking up a dust cloud behind them. The taller of the two boys had close-cropped brown hair. The other had copper-colored hair and freckles.

"There go the Three Musketeers," said the tall boy, scratching his crew cut.

"How come they never ask us to go on any of their adventures, Billy?" asked the red-haired boy, squinting to keep track of the dust cloud in the distance.

"I guess we're not cool enough to hang out with the

smart kids, Fred," Billy replied sarcastically. "Want to follow them?"

"Excellent idea, Billy," Fred replied, a smirk spreading across his freckled face. "Let's move!" he exclaimed, imitating Rad's cry.

As the research center faded from view, Rad, Carlos, and Alexis made their way up into the mountains a short distance from their homes. The three friends didn't exactly love living on a government base, but it was the only life they had ever known. Each of the three had moved to the Cosmo Center when they were infants. They figured growing up in a big city or even in a real town would have been more interesting, but they always managed to make the best of being Cosmo Kids.

And they had each other. The three shared a love of fast-moving vehicles, radical moves, and a strong sense of adventure. They had always found ways to make their own fun, and today would be no different.

Reaching a familiar stretch of the mountain trail they often rode, Rad looked over his shoulder at his two friends. "Ready for the crisscross?" he called back.

Carlos and Alexis flashed him a thumbs up sign.

"Go!" Rad shouted, riding his bike up the side of a smooth, steeply sloped rock face. Peddling hard, gaining speed, he yanked up on the handlebars and launched himself into the air.

At the same moment, Carlos steered his skateboard onto a sloping bank on the side of the trail. Sailing into the air, he squatted low, grabbing the front of his skateboard with one hand, using the other for balance, just as Rad flew over his head.

As Rad headed back toward the ground, Alexis pushed off on her scooter. Rolling along a ledge just above the boys, she took off, sailing over Rad's head, seconds after Carlos had passed under him.

"Extreme!" Alexis shouted as she landed.

"Radical!" Rad yelled, lifting both fists into the air.

"Awesome, guys!" Carlos added, executing his favorite sideways stop, then flipping his board up into his hand.

The three friends continued along the mountain path, practicing new extreme moves, sliding down hills, and bouncing off boulders. When they had almost reached the top of the mountain, Rad spotted a trail he had never noticed before.

"Check this out," he called to the others as he skidded to a stop. He pointed at the narrow trail leading up and around the mountain. "I don't know this trail. Let's see where it leads."

Carlos and Alexis nodded, then followed Rad up the mountain path.

"Cool," said Alexis. Then in a mock TV announcer's

voice she added "Welcome to *The Cosmo Kids Explore New Territory,* 'Episode One: 'The Unknown Trail.'"

Rolling along single file, the friends wound up and around the steep path. This side of the mountain was mostly in the shade, and they could feel the temperature drop as they reached a second trail. It was even narrower than the one they were on. This trail branched off to the left. At the point where the two trails met, a painted wooden sign stuck out of the ground.

"Oooh," Rad moaned in a fake scary voice. "Look at this. It says 'DANGER! FALLING ROCKS! KEEP OUT!' Sounds like an invitation to me." Then imitating Alexis's announcer voice he added, "'Episode Two: The Sign the Cosmo Kids Ignored.' Come on."

Carlos shook his head. "I don't know about this," he said seriously. "It could be dangerous. I mean, it does say 'danger!'"

"Maybe we should stick to the trails we know," Alexis added, biting her lower lip nervously.

"Bor-ing," Rad said in a sing-song voice. "I have a good feeling about this. Come on, guys. Trust me."

Looking at each other for a moment, then shrugging, Carlos and Alexis followed Rad onto the narrow trail.

Chapter 2

The Cave
of Darkness

Rad, Carlos, and Alexis followed the trail until they came to the base of a tall mountain peak. In front of them was a pile of rocks, the result of a rock slide.

"I guess the sign wasn't kidding about the falling rocks," Alexis said, jumping off her scooter and leaning it against a nearby tree.

Carlos leaped from his skateboard, setting it next to Alexis's scooter. Rad lifted himself into another handlebar handstand, then pushed himself off, executing a perfect dismount. Hoisting his bike over his head, Rad placed it alongside the skateboard and scooter.

"Look at this," Carlos called out as he climbed onto the rock pile. "There's a small opening here. I think these rocks are covering the entrance to a cave."

Alexis and Rad quickly joined Carlos. All three peered into a thin crack between the rocks. Cool air

rushed from the opening. Picking up a small stone, Rad tossed it into the crevice. The sound of the pebble bouncing on the solid rock echoed softly.

"You're right!" Rad exclaimed, pulling a flashlight from his backpack.

"'Episode Three: The Cave of Darkness,'" Alexis said in her TV announcer's voice.

Switching on the flashlight, Rad turned sideways and squeezed through the slender opening. The others slipped through the crevice, following Rad into the cave.

Darkness immediately surrounded them. The cave felt cold and damp, and the ground was hard and slippery. Rad swept his flashlight beam around in the darkness, revealing a room with a high ceiling. Tunnels led from the room in several directions.

"This is really creepy," said Carlos, shivering as a chill ran down his spine.

"Hey," said Rad as he focused his beam on the largest tunnel. "You wanted adventure. You got it. Follow me."

Sticking close together, the three friends entered the large tunnel. Rad led the way, lighting their path. Carlos kept one hand on the slimy wall, so he wouldn't get caught by surprise if the tunnel took a sharp turn. Alexis brought up the rear, squinting ahead into the darkness.

"It feels like we're heading lower!" she said. Alexis

realized she was picking up speed, so she slowed down to avoid bumping into Carlos.

"It's certainly getting colder," Carlos said, feeling the dampness seep into his sneakers.

Down they went, further and further into the tunnel.

"At this rate, we could end up in China," Alexis joked after they had been trudging along for twenty minutes.

"Hold it," said Rad, sticking out his hand to stop the others. "It looks like the tunnel opens up into some kind of cavern up ahead. Come on."

The friends picked up their pace, walking quickly toward the cavern. When they got there, Rad's flashlight revealed an enormous open chamber with an extremely high ceiling.

"Wow!" cried Rad, his voice echoing in the cavern. "You could fit the entire school in here."

"Yeah," agreed Alexis. "But it would be a little tough to read the board with just a flashlight."

Rad slowly explored the walls of the cavern with his beam. When the circle of light struck the wall on the far side of the cave, the three friends let out a gasp.

"Pictures!" shouted Carlos. "Look! There are pictures on that wall."

"I guess we're not the first kids to find this cave," Rad said as the three kids gazed at the wall.

"Who would be so rude to come into this cave and

scribble graffiti all over the walls?" Alexis asked. She was outraged at the thought that anyone would do something so childish.

Rad stopped and turned toward Alexis. "Billy and Fred!" the three friends all said at the same time.

"I can't believe they found this place before us," Carlos said, shaking his head.

"Me, neither," Rad agreed. "But if they did, I wouldn't put it past them to scribble dumb drawings on the wall. Come on, let's take a closer look."

****

Back outside, at the point where Rad, Carlos, and Alexis had found the new trail, Billy and Fred were straddling their bikes. They looked down at the marks on the ground left by the tires and wheels of Rad's bike, Carlos' skateboard, and Alexis' scooter.

"Looks like they headed up that way," Fred said, pointing at the narrow path.

"You ever been up that trail?" Billy asked.

"Nope," Fred replied. "But if those guys can make it up the mountain, we can, too."

"I'm with you, pal," said Billy. "Let's go find out what they're up to." The two boys pedaled hard up the steep trail, hoping to find Rad, Carlos, and Alexis.

Billy and Fred had moved to the Cosmo Scope Research Center only a few years ago. Not having grown up there, like most of the other kids, they always felt like outsiders. They were not really bad kids, they just didn't fit in with the others.

Billy spent the first nine years of his life growing up in a big city. When his mother was offered the opportunity to live and work at the Interstellar Observatory, she jumped at the chance. Billy was very upset about leaving his friends, his school, and his life in the city. He disliked living "in the middle of nowhere," as he called it. He quickly gained a reputation as a tough kid, who didn't fit in.

Fred grew up in the suburbs with parents who spent most of their time working. Always a below-average student, Fred was struggling at the Cosmo school. He sometimes felt embarrassed trying to hang out with the smart kids, as he called Rad, Carlos, and Alexis.

At first, the three Cosmo Kids invited Billy and Fred along on their adventures. But Billy and Fred proved to be bossy, always telling the others what to do and where to go. And they argued all the time. Eventually, Rad, Carlos, and Alexis decided they preferred not to hang out with Billy and Fred. This made the boys feel even more like outsiders.

Why should those three have all the fun? Billy

thought. *We can go wherever we want.* It just so happened that where they usually wanted to go was exactly where Rad, Carlos, and Alexis went. Today was no different.

Billy and Fred soon reached the warning sign where the trail branched off.

"Falling rocks!" cried Fred, reading the sign. "They'd have to be crazy to go up there."

"Well, it looks like they did," Billy said pointing to the tracks on the trail.

"I don't know, Billy," Fred said nervously. "The sign says 'Danger!'"

"Are you chicken?" Billy asked accusingly. "You afraid of a little sign? Well, I'm going up. You can do what you want."

"Alright! Alright!" Fred whined. "I'm coming." Up they rode along the bumpy trail. When they reached the pile of rocks at the base of the mountain peak, Billy spotted the bike, skateboard, and scooter that the other kids had left outside the cave.

"They must have walked from here," he said. "But where did they go? Their footprints lead right to that big pile of rocks."

Leaning their bikes against a tree, Billy and Fred climbed onto the rocks.

"I think there's a small opening that leads into a

cave," Fred announced.

Billy pulled a flashlight from his backpack. "That's where they are," he said, shining his light into the narrow crack. "Come on. Let's go explore."

"I don't know, Billy," Fred grumbled. "What if there's another rock slide? Or maybe there's some kind of animal living in there? Or what if—"

"I see an animal right here," Billy shot back. "A chicken. *Buck-buck-buck*. Or maybe it's a scaredy cat."

"Don't call me chicken!" Fred yelled.

"Then come with me!" Billy shouted.

"Ok, but if something bad happens—"

"Nothing bad is going to happen," Billy barked at his friend. "Don't be such a baby!"

"I'm not a baby!" Fred shouted.

Billy led the way through the narrow entrance into the cave. In the narrow beam of Billy's flashlight, the two boys saw that they were in a large room with many tunnels branching off.

"Where do we go now, Billy?" Fred asked.

"Let's take that big tunnel," Billy replied, waving his light toward the largest tunnel. Taking a step forward, Billy slipped on the slick rocks and fell hard. His flashlight hit the ground and went off.

"Billy!" Fred cried, as panic set in.

"Stop yelling!" Billy called out. "I'm okay." Groping

along the ground in the darkness, he found his flashlight. Switching it on, he scrambled to his feet.

"Maybe we should get out of here," Fred suggested.

"Come on," Billy said. "Let's go a little way into that tunnel and see what's up ahead."

"Alright," Fred agreed, rubbing his cold hands together. "I guess a little way would be okay."

With Fred following closely behind him, Billy led the way into the tunnel.

Chapter 3

Mini-con Robots Revealed

Rad, Carlos, and Alexis stared in amazement at the pictures on the cavern wall. They quickly realized that the drawings were not the scribblings of mischievous kids.

"They look like cave paintings," Alexis said. "The kind done by primitive people thousands of years ago."

"Except these aren't pictures of cavemen sitting around a fire," Rad pointed out, "or hunting buffalo."

"Yeah!" Carlos exclaimed, his eyes wide. "These are cool paintings of giant robots fighting!"

Rad swept his flashlight beam across the wall. There was a series of rectangular paintings lined up along the wall like panels in a comic book. The images showed an epic battle between two armies of giant robots.

Some robots had arms, legs, heads, and bodies. Others looked like giant machines—tanks, planes, and rocket ships. Robots battled in hand-to-hand combat while others blasted laser rays at their enemies. Images of giant spaceships lit up star-filled skies, telling the tale of a great space battle high above a metallic planet. In the center of the battle, two robots, both bigger than all the others, grappled in a life or death struggle.

"This tells the story of some kind of robot war," Rad said, shaking his head. "I wonder where it took place?"

"Obviously not on Earth!" Alexis said, pointing to one painting. "That planet looks like it's made of metal."

"Giant robots from a metal planet?" Carlos said excitedly. "Awesome!" He thought for moment then asked the question that all three kids had been wondering about.

"What are these pictures doing here, buried in a cave on Earth?" he asked.

"Good question," Alexis said.

Moving along the wall, the three kids came to the final three paintings. These featured images of three robots, smaller than the rest. These robots didn't seem to be battling anyone.

"They're kind of cute," Alexis said.

The two boys looked at her and groaned.

"Well they are!" Alexis said somewhat defensively. "Just look at them."

Stepping closer to the wall, each of the kids moved toward the image of one of the three smaller robots. As if driven by some unknown, unseen force, all three reached out at the same moment to touch one of the three drawings.

Instantly, the wall began to glow with an eerie, pulsating light. The ground suddenly shook and several small rocks tumbled down from above.

"Rock slide!" Carlos shouted, terrified. "Maybe we should get out of here."

"No," Rad said. He couldn't say why, but he was absolutely certain they weren't in any danger. "It's OK. I'm sure of it. Let's get under that outcropping and wait out the rock slide."

Alexis and Carlos quickly agreed. They didn't know why but they, too, suddenly felt they would be safe under the outcropping. Huddled together under a thick ledge, the three friends watched as a shower of pebbles and stones fell from above. The wall before them continued to glow.

****

Further back up the tunnel, Billy and Fred were panicking. The narrow walls on either side of them shook. Small rocks tumbled down, bouncing at their feet. As they often did when they were frightened, they began arguing with each other.

"I told you we shouldn't have come in here!" Fred

shouted. "But you always have to be such a big shot!"

"Shut up!" Billy cried, turning and running back up the tunnel. "You said it was okay to come in here, too!"

"Did not!" Fred yelled, hurrying to keep up with Billy and his flashlight beam. "Now we're going to die in an earthquake or a rock slide or whatever this is!"

"No one is going to die!" Billy screamed at his friend. "Just hurry up!"

The pair scrambled back up the tunnel into the large entry room. They quickly squeezed out through the narrow crack and found themselves outside.

"There, we made it!" Billy shouted. "Happy now?"

"What about those guys?" Fred asked pointing at the bike, skateboard, and scooter that were leaning near their own bikes.

"I'll bet they never even went in there!" Billy said as he and Fred picked up their bikes and headed back down the mountain trail. "They're probably just off in the woods somewhere taking a walk. After all, who would be stupid enough to go into a place like that!"

"Yeah," Fred agreed. "Who would be stupid enough to go in there?" Then the two friends rode home without saying another word.

****

The cave continued rumbling and shaking, and rocks continued to fall, as Rad, Carlos, and Alexis pressed together under the overhanging ledge.

"Look!" shouted Alexis, pointing to the paintings. "Something's happening to the wall."

The three watched in amazement as the wall of paintings rose like a curtain, sliding up into the ceiling of the cavern, revealing an enormous metal chamber behind it. When the wall had vanished from view, the rock slide ended. The ground stopped shaking and the cave grew silent.

Scrambling to their feet, the three friends stepped forward into the metal chamber. Control panels and view screens lined the room's high walls. Sleek lighting fixtures ran the length of the dented metal ceiling.

"This is the inside of a spaceship!" Carlos cried gazing at the high-tech equipment all around him. "I'm sure of it!"

"It certainly does look like a spaceship," Alexis agreed. "But whose?"

As if in answer to Alexis's question, three rectangular panels rose out of the floor. On each panel was an image of one of the smaller robots the kids had seen earlier.

"It looks like your cute little robots are back!" Rad

teased Alexis.

Before she could respond, Alexis and the others watched as the three panels began to glow, brighter and brighter. It got so bright the children had to shield their eyes. When the glowing stopped, the three robots pictured on the panel were standing there, as real as the startled children who stared at them in disbelief.

The small robots were no bigger than the three kids. They rotated their heads, their mechanical eyes lighting up as they looked around.

The robot closest to Rad let out a high-pitched electronic noise. "*Breeee-oooopt!*" it said.

"He says his name is High Wire," Rad translated.

"You understood what he said?" Carlos asked. To him it sounded like a series of squeaks and tones.

"*Verpeeeeediiiii*," said the robot near Carlos.

"This one is called Grindor," Carlos explained. "Somehow I can understand him."

"But I can't!" Rad pointed out. "I could understand the first one though. This is so weird."

Alexis looked closely at the robot next to her. "What's your name?" she asked.

"*Zaaaaaatweeedeeeteeedee!*" screeched the robot. "*Muuuuiiiiooo!*"

"Her name is Sureshock," Alexis said. "And they are called Mini-cons."

"That one's a girl?" Carlos asked.

"Sure," Alexis replied. "Why not?"

Over the next few minutes, the three friends realized that they could each understand one of the Mini-cons, but not the others. They each felt a special connection to one of the robots.

When they got over the shock of seeing robots, the three kids began to pepper the Mini-cons with questions. The answers they got amazed them. From their new friends, the children learned about the planet Cybertron and of the great war between the Autobots and the Decepticons. The Mini-cons told how both sides had fought over control of the Mini-cons, and how the Mini-cons were launched into space. The kids learned that these three robots were the first Mini-cons to awaken after millions of years of laying buried in this cave.

"So that's what all those cave paintings mean!" Carlos exclaimed.

"Exactly," Grindor replied in his own language, though only Carlos understood him. "They tell of the great war on Cybertron. This chamber you see all around you is the spaceship that brought us to Earth."

"I knew it was a spaceship!" Carlos exclaimed.

Suddenly, the ship began to shake and rumble. Lights on the ceiling suddenly flared into brightness. A low humming noise filled the cave and grew louder as the ship powered up. Energy surged through its long-dormant circuits. Equipment all around the chamber lit up and beeped, as the powerful spaceship came to life.

The warp gate mechanism, placed in the ship long ago, activated. The children watched in stunned amazement as three beams of light began to materialize.

A red beam and a purple beam shot out from the ship, bathing the kids and the Mini-cons in dazzling, laser-like light. The beams grew thicker, then traveled out of the cave and up into the vastness of space. The beams continued on through space until they finally reached the surface of the planet Cybertron.

A glowing, green beam also shot out of the ship and struck Earth's moon. The green beam activated the part of the Mini-con spaceship that had crashed there millions of years ago. The beam then broke up into many segments, each one striking a Mini-con buried on the moon. Another segment of the beam hit the moon's surface and split into even more segments that bounced back to Earth. Each segment struck a Mini-con somewhere on Earth.

The kids were awestruck. They'd never seen anything like it. "What's going on, High Wire?" Rad asked the Mini-con.

High Wire studied the beams carefully. Then he spoke. "They are coming," he said.

"Who's coming?" Rad asked.

"The Autobots and the Decepticons," High Wire explained. "The warp gate has opened. The red and purple beams will transport them."

"Transport them where?" Rad asked nervously.

High Wire studied the beams for a moment. Then he turned to the three kids.

"Here," High Wire replied. "To Earth."

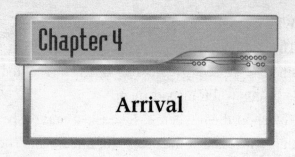

Chapter 4

Arrival

On the planet Cybertron, war was raging out of control. The forces of the Autobots who believed in peace, liberty, and knowledge battled the Decepticons, who craved only power and domination over others.

Peace had lasted for many years once the Mini-cons were launched into space. But eventually Megatron, the leader of the Decepticons, decided it was time once again to seize control of the planet. Once Cybertron was firmly in his grasp, he would move on and conquer other worlds. His ultimate ambition was to one day rule the entire universe.

Standing in his way was Optimus Prime, a great warrior and leader of the Autobots. Thanks to Optimus Prime's leadership, the Autobots managed to keep the Decepticons from gaining control of Cybertron.

Just outside Cybertron's largest city, Optimus Prime and Megatron struggled in a titanic battle that would determine which side gained control of the city and its vast resources.

In their robot forms, both combatants resembled giant mechanical men. Standing over twenty feet tall, each of their arms and legs was a huge and powerful weapon on its own. Each leader was a super fighting machine with devastating destructive abilities.

"This city will be mine!" Megatron bellowed, unleashing a mighty punch aimed right at Optimus Prime's head.

"You will never gain control of the city!" Optimus Prime vowed, as he caught Megatron's fist in his own powerful hand. Pushing forward, Optimus Prime sent Megatron flying into the side of an abandoned building on the edge of the city.

The impact made the teetering building tumble down onto Megatron. Buried in the rubble for mere seconds, the furious Decepticon leader burst from the pile of steel and glass, spraying debris in all directions.

"You cannot stop me, Optimus Prime!" Megatron blustered. "I have waited four million years to gain control of Cybertron. I will wait four million more if I must. This planet will be mine!"

As strong as both the Decepticons and the Autobots were in their robot forms, they possessed an amazing ability, which made them even more powerful. Both types of Transformers could change their shape. They could reconfigure themselves, morphing into machines or vehicles. Once this transformation was complete, the robots took on the characteristics and powers of whatever they transformed into.

"TRANSFORM!" Megatron shouted.

As Optimus Prime braced himself for the next onslaught, Megatron transformed into a giant flame thrower, an extremely powerful military weapon. His arms swung around in front of him, snapping into place to form a long cannon-like weapon. His legs spun sideways, morphing into thick, all-terrain wheels.

"TRANSFORM!" Optimus Prime shouted, knowing he had to counter Megatron's move with a transformation of his own.

The Autobot leader transformed into a powerful-looking spaceship, his head spreading wide to form a thick heat shield in front. His body compacted, and the bottoms of his feet opened to reveal rocket thrusters.

Megatron shot a wall of fire from his cannon-like flame thrower. The rush of fire washed over Optimus Prime. The heat shield on the front of his spaceship form deflected the flames, protecting the Autobot leader.

Firing his rocket engine, Optimus Prime blasted off and few through the air. Seconds later he slammed into the flame thrower form of Megatron.

Stunned from the impact, both combatants transformed back into their robot forms, and prepared for the next attack. All around them, Autobots and Decepticons battled. Some fought in robot form. Others transformed into vehicles, machines, construction equipment, and weapons of war. The city was already hovering on the brink of total disaster. Now, as the battle moved closer, it threatened to destroy everything that stood in it.

Optimus Prime and Megatron rose to their feet. Glaring at each other, both robots rushed forward, ready for the latest in their endless series of clashes.

Suddenly two brilliant beams of light poured down from the sky. A red beam struck Optimus Prime, surrounding him with a crimson glow and freezing him in his tracks. The beam grew wider, covering many other Autobots. Then Optimus Prime and his loyal Autobot soldiers vanished, the red beam disappearing into the clear blue sky.

"You cannot hide from me, Optimus Prime!" Megatron yelled. Then a purple beam surrounded Megatron and his Decepticon army. The purple beam suddenly vanished, transporting Megatron and his troops away from Cybertron.

Back on Earth, deep inside the mountain cave, Rad, Carlos, and Alexis introduced themselves to the Mini-cons. In turn, they learned more about their new robot friends. The three kids were amazed that they had found a four-million-year-old spaceship, and were thrilled that they had somehow helped bring these friendly robots back to life.

High Wire, Grindor, and Sureshock told the three friends the entire story of the great war that had taken place on Cybertron. They explained the role the Mini-cons played, and they described the power of the Autobots and the Decepticons.

The children found much of this confusing and hard to believe. It all seemed so unreal. Still, here they were in a cave in a mountain, miles from their homes, talking to robots in a giant buried spaceship. At the moment, anything seemed possible.

Rad was still concerned about High Wire's explanation of the colored beams which had shot out from the ship.

"Why would the Autobots and Decepticons come here?" he asked.

"Before they launched us on our journey," High Wire began, "they built a warp gate device in our spaceship. This device was programmed to transport both the

Autobots and the Decepticons to our location if anyone discovered us. They feared that other civilizations would fight over our abilities, and they hoped to avoid wars on other planets."

"So these guys stopped their war when they sent you Mini-cons into space?" Rad asked.

"That is correct," High Wire replied.

Since each of the three friends could understand only their own Mini-con, and not the others, much time was spent explaining and translating, until Rad, Carlos, and Alexis had all pieced together this incredible story.

Suddenly, the entire cave shook. The sounds of shouting, explosions, and metal clashing against metal came pouring in from the tunnel.

"Something's going on outside!" Carlos cried.

"They have arrived," Grindor said.

Rad, Carlos, and Alexis raced back through the large tunnel, followed closely by High Wire, Grindor, and Sureshock. Reaching the large entry room, they quickly slipped through the narrow crack and climbed out through the pile of fallen rocks.

When the three friends and their Mini-cons emerged from the cave, they were greeted by a sight almost too incredible to believe. Nothing the Mini-cons had told them could have prepared the kids for the scene taking place just outside the cave.

All around them giant robots battled. The Autobots and Decepticons—transported from Cybertron by the Mini-cons' beams—were continuing their war on Earth, right in front of Rad, Carlos, and Alexis.

"I thought you said their war was over!" Rad said to High Wire, as he watched armies of robots, all kinds of vehicles, and machines wage a fierce battle.

"Apparently," High Wire began in a flat, emotionless robotic voice, "the Autobots and Decepticons are waging war once again."

"Yeah!" Rad cried. "And this time, it's right here in our very own backyard!"

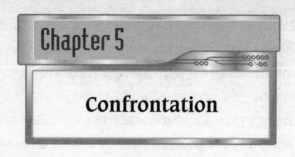

Chapter 5

Confrontation

The Autobots and Decepticons continued to fight intensely. Explosions shattered the quiet mountainside, as pieces of damaged robots flew into rocks and trees and burst into flame.

These robot soldiers had been trained not to question anything—including the fact that they had been suddenly pulled from their home planet to fight on a distant alien world.

Caught up in their age-old battle, the Autobots and Decepticons didn't notice the three children and three Mini-cons who now looked on from the cave entrance.

At least, not for the moment.

When they stepped from the cave, the Mini-cons immediately spotted Rad's BMX bike, Carlos' skateboard, and Alexis' scooter, still leaning against the tree where they had left them.

Beeping with excitement, High Wire, Grindor, and

Sureshock hurried over to the vehicles. Mini-cons were amazed by these unfamiliar vehicles, which were unlike anything they had ever encountered on Cybertron. The Mini-cons, like all Transformers had the same ability to change their shape into any vehicle they happened to see. As their new human friends looked on with astonishment, the Mini-cons underwent an amazing transformation.

"TRANSFORM!" High Wire said, taking on the form of a super, high-tech BMX bike. Thin streaks of light ran along his frame and handlebars, lighting up the sleek machine.

"TRANSFORM!" Grindor yelled, reconfiguring himself into a glittering metal skateboard with large, glowing wheels.

"TRANSFORM!" cried Sureshock, morphing herself into a shimmering motorized chrome scooter, covered in flashing lights.

Rad, Carlos, and Alexis ran over to the Mini-cons, astounded by their transformation.

"High Wire," Rad began, doing his trademark handlebar handstand, landing on the seat. "You are definitely the coolest BMX bike ever!"

"Check out this skateboard!" Carlos cried, jumping onto the gleaming metal board, spinning on its back wheels. "Grindor, you rule!"

Hopping onto Sureshock in her scooter form, Alexis revved the engine. Sureshock zoomed in a circle around the other two Mini-cons. "Wow!" she shouted. "You are supercharged, Sureshock!"

The three Mini-cons skidded to a stop in front of the entrance to the cave. Suddenly an enormous shadow loomed over the three friends and their Mini-cons.

Towering over them was a giant robot, its evil eyes glaring down at the six tiny figures before it.

"I recognize him from the cave painting!" Rad whispered to the others. "He's one of the robots fighting in that big battle scene."

"That is Megatron," High Wire explained, "leader of the Decepticons."

"So," Megatron boomed, staring at the three transformed Mini-cons. "After all these millions of years the Mini-cons have awakened! The warp gate we placed in your ship has done its job. And it could not have happened at a better time. You can see, the war between the Decepticons and the Autobots has resumed. However, once I take control of the Mini-cons, this conflict will quickly come to an end—with the Decepticons as the victors!"

All around the battlefield, Autobots and Decepticons whispered in amazement, pointing at the Mini-cons. For most Transformers, the Mini-cons were only a myth, a legend from their planet's distant past. They now realized that the ancient tales they had heard were indeed true. The Mini-cons had returned to life, here on this planet called Earth.

"And now I will take these Mini-cons," the evil Megatron boasted, stepping toward the children and their robot friends.

"What do we do now?' Carlos asked, backing up.

All three friends had their backs pressed against the sheer face of the mountain. They were trapped, with no apparent escape route.

The kids stood frozen as Megatron reached down with his massive metallic hand.

"You will not take those Mini-cons, Megatron!" a voice boomed from behind the giant robot. A huge metal hand grabbed Megatron's shoulder, yanking him away from the kids and the Mini-cons.

"Hey!" Carlos cried. "That's the other giant robot from the cave painting!"

"That is Optimus Prime," Grindor explained to Carlos. "He is the leader of the Autobots."

"Optimus Prime!" Megatron bellowed. "You did not defeat me on Cybertron, and you will not defeat me on this insignificant little planet!"

Megatron grabbed Optimus Prime by the arm and hurled him away. As he flew through the air, Optimus

Prime extended his arm, lengthening it just enough to grab Megatron by the ankle. The Decepticon leader fell onto his back, as Optimus Prime dragged him along the rocky ground.

"Capture those Mini-cons!" Megatron screamed as he struggled to regain his footing. "That is a direct order!"

Instantly, all the Decepticons stopped their battles and turned their attention to the three Mini-cons. A troop of Decepticons, robots and vehicles alike, rushed toward the Mini-cons and the three children who had befriended them.

"What now?" Alexis asked, trembling.

"I don't know," Carlos replied, frozen with fear.

"I'm open to any suggestions, guys," Rad added. "But we'd better think of something fast. Those robots will be on us in a couple of seconds!"

As if answering the children's questions, the three Mini-cons took off under their own power and raced away from the onrushing Decepticons. Rad, Carlos, and Alexis hung on for dear life.

"Whoa!" cried Rad as High Wire sped away from the cave, followed closely by Grindor and Sureshock. "I'm not even pedaling!"

"That is not necessary," High Wire pointed out. "I will supply the power for our forward motion. You just hold on tightly, please."

"And I will operate your skateboard," Grindor said, as Carlos zoomed along with the wind whipping through his dark, curly hair.

"I always wondered what it would be like to put a motor on my skateboard," Carlos said. "But this is better than I ever imagined."

"Grasp the handlebars firmly, please," Sureshock said to Alexis.

"You bet!" Alexis shouted as Sureshock raced after the other Mini-cons.

"This is awesome!" Carlos yelled, his arms extended and his knees bent for balance. Lost in the excitement of the ride, he had practically forgotten about the dangerous robots pursuing them.

"Hey, I think you are forgetting something, Carlos!" Alexis shouted.

"What?" Carlos asked.

"Them!" Alexis yelled her reply, pointing back.

A squadron of Decepticons was closing in.

"Where should we go?" Rad cried out.

"We can't head home," Alexis said, pulling out Rover, her handheld computer, and switching on the GPS. "I don't want to lead these robots to the complex!"

"It doesn't look like we have any say in the matter," Rad pointed out. "These Mini-cons are in control. Where are they taking us?"

"According to my GPS," Alexis said, checking Rover's tiny monitor, "they're taking us back to the cave where we found them!"

"That is correct, Alexis," Sureshock said. "Our sensors indicate that the Decepticons are planning to enter the cave to capture our ship. We cannot allow that to happen."

Rolling and bouncing along the rugged terrain, the Mini-cons circled their way back to the cave entrance, slowing to a stop. The three friends jumped off the vehicles and watched as the Decepticons closed in on them. The kids stood by, helpless.

Or so it seemed.

Moving swiftly, the three Mini-cons underwent a second incredible transformation. Grindor leaped onto High Wire's back fender, attaching himself to the BMX bike. Then Sureshock connected herself High Wire's handlebars, as the three Mini-cons joined together to form one single robot.

The combined Mini-cons began glowing with a bright golden aura.

Seeing this, Optimus Prime shoved Megatron away, then raced to the Mini-cons' side.

The Mini-cons' glow began to grow in both size and intensity. It quickly formed a protective energy dome that surrounded the three children, Optimus Prime, and the cave containing the Mini-con spaceship.

"What is this?" Megatron blustered. "Do you think some display of lights can stop the mighty Megatron?"

Megatron raced forward, slamming into the protective energy dome with all his vast strength.

FOOOOING!

The giant robot bounced off the golden shield and fell sprawling to the ground. "Impossible!" he bellowed. Scrambling to his feet, Megatron dashed at the dome for another try.

FOOOOING!

Again he was repelled. Following two more vain attempts to break through the Mini-cons' dome, Megatron quickly formulated a back-up plan. Scanning the atmosphere for energy signatures, he picked up traces of the green beam which had struck the moon.

"Ah!" he said, an evil smile spreading across his gleaming face. "There is another section of the Mini-con ship on Earth's moon! If I cannot claim this one, then perhaps the one on the moon will serve me better."

Glaring through the energy dome at his ancient adversary, Megatron continued.

"Optimus Prime!" he bellowed. "You have won this battle, but the war will go on. I will return and capture not just these three Mini-cons, but all the Mini-cons on Earth. I will then use them to increase the power of the

Decepticons to defeat you once and for all!"

Megatron signaled his fellow Decepticons, then activated a warp gate built into his robotic armor. A surge of power surrounded the Decepticon leader, then spread out, covering his troops. With a blinding flash, Megatron and the Decepticons suddenly vanished.

Chapter 6

Fortress of the Autobots

Optimus Prime stared out through the yellow haze of the Mini-cons' protective energy dome. Using the long range scanners built into his robotic eyes, he searched the entire area around the cave, but found no sign of any Decepticons.

"So, Megatron was telling the truth," he said, looking down at the Mini-cons. "The Decepticons have left this planet...for the moment."

Hearing this, the Mini-cons shut down their protective force field. Then the three individual robots separated, quickly transforming into Grindor, High Wire, and Sureshock.

Optimus Prime looked down at the trio of tiny robots before him. "Never did I believe that I would again set eyes on the Mini-cons," he said sadly. "For I knew that if I did, it would lead to yet another destructive conflict with the Decepticons."

"*Vreet-oop pipa*," High Wire beeped, looking at Rad.

"Yeah, High Wire, I'm fine," Rad replied. "Thanks to you, Grindor, and Sureshock."

Optimus Prime turned to the human children for the first time. "You understand the language of this Mini-con?" he asked Rad.

"Sure," replied Rad.

"And I understand Grindor," Carlos added.

"Sureshock and I are already old friends," Alexis said, squeezing the handlebars of Sureshock's motor scooter form. "Aren't we, pal?"

"*Beeeetriiiii!*" Sureshock trilled her agreement.

Rad looked up at Optimus Prime. The huge robot was a little frightening, not looking all that different from the evil Megatron. But somehow the three friends sensed that he meant them no harm. "Can't you understand them?" Rad asked Autobot leader.

"I cannot," he replied softly. "Long ago, when my Autobot brothers and sisters used the Mini-cons, we regarded them as tools. We did not even know they were capable of communication. Apparently, much has changed since the time they were launched into space from the planet Cybertron.

"Unfortunately, what has not changed is the Decepticons' desire to capture and control the Mini-cons, and to use them to achieve their goals of conquest and domination. I fear that the warp gate device we built into their ship has transported our ancient war to your innocent planet."

"They've got a really cool ship," Carlos blurted out.

"What?" Optimus Prime cried out in shock. "You have seen the Mini-cons' spaceship?"

"Sure," replied Alexis, pointing to the tiny entrance to the cave. "It's right in there. Only I don't think you'll fit through the narrow opening in those rocks."

"This is a stroke of luck!" Optimus Prime exclaimed, his voice brightening with hope. "Perhaps we Autobots can use the Mini-cons' ship as a fortress, a home base for the coming war here on Earth. I must see the Mini-cons' ship at once."

The children and their Mini-cons stepped aside and watched in amazement. Optimus Prime easily lifted the heavy boulders from the massive pile of rocks at the front of the cave. He tossed them aside, one by one, as if they were tiny pebbles. When he had cleared away the entire pile, the Autobot leader stared into the large curved entryway which led into the cave.

"I'll have to fashion some type of door mechanism if this is to be our main defensive position," he announced. "But first, please lead me to the Mini-cons' ship."

High Wire, Grindor, and Sureshock reconfigured themselves back to their robot forms. Lighting the path with bright searchlights built into their mechanical bodies, the three Mini-cons led the way into the cave, through the large tunnel, and into their spaceship.

All around, equipment onboard flashed and hummed. The ship pulsated with robotic life, once again fully functional.

"This is magnificent!" Optimus Prime declared as he looked over the control panels, communications, and weapons systems. "This ship has all the necessary technology to help us make a stand on this planet against the Decepticons. It shall be our fortress in the coming battles."

A sudden change of expression came over Optimus Prime's face. The giant robot seemed to be embarrassed. Bending down so that his head was at the same level as those of the Mini-cons, he spoke directly to the tiny robots. "That is," he began, "if it is all right with the Mini-cons. This is, after all, your ship."

All three Mini-cons beeped, screeched, and clicked.

"High Wire says he would be honored if you would use his ship as a base if it will help you stop the Decepticons," Rad translated.

"Yes," Carlos added. "Grindor says that the Decepticons have always treated the Mini-cons cruelly. He would be happy to help the Autobots."

A look of concern spread over Alexis's face.

"Sureshock agrees," she reported. "However, she asked me to remind you, Optimus Prime, that if a Decepticon discovers a Mini-con first and reactivates it, that Mini-con will have no choice but to serve the Decepticon who found it."

"I understand," said Optimus Prime. Then he began the task of cleaning up the rubble from the rock slide, and setting up the Mini-con ship as his fortress.

"We've got to get out of here!" Rad exclaimed suddenly, looking at his watch. "Our folks are going to start to worry if we don't get home soon."

"Wow!" Carlos exclaimed looking at his watch. "Time sure flies when you're fighting Decepticons. We'd better move it."

"Don't worry, Optimus Prime," Alexis said. "We'll keep your presence on Earth a secret. By the way, my name is Alexis."

"Thank you, Alexis," Optimus Prime replied. "I am sorry you and your world had to get involved."

"My name is Brad," Rad stated. "But everyone calls me Rad. I'm the leader of this little group."

"No way!" Carlos shouted. "Just because you're the oldest? Get a grip." Then turning to Optimus Prime, he added, "I'm Carlos, and Rad here is nuts!"

Optimus Prime looked at the children and smiled. "Perhaps we will meet again, Rad, Carlos, Alexis."

"You can count on it!" Rad said, turning to leave. As the three kids headed away from the ship, Optimus Prime was surprised to see the Mini-cons following Rad, Carlos, and Alexis. "Will the Mini-cons be going home with you?" Optimus Prime asked, a puzzled look on his face.

High Wire squeaked a reply.

"High Wire says that he and Grindor and Sureshock feel a strong connection with the three of us," Rad translated. "They choose to stay by our side."

Optimus Prime nodded. "As Transformers, they are free to choose their own fate," he explained.

"And we're really happy to have them!" Carlos said with glee.

"Don't worry, Optimus Prime," Alexis said. "We'll take good care of them."

"I'm sure you will," Optimus Prime replied.

Rad, Carlos, and Alexis left the cave, followed by the three Mini-cons. As Rad, Carlos, and Alexis retrieved their bike, skateboard, and scooter, their Mini-cons transformed back into their vehicle forms. The kids pulled their old vehicles along as they rode their new Mini-con vehicles home.

"What'll we tell our folks about these new vehicles?" Carlos asked, realizing that there would have to be some explanation for the sudden appearance of his souped-up, super-cool skateboard.

"Let's just say we won them in an extreme riding contest," Alexis suggested as she zoomed along on Sureshock, who beeped her approval for the idea.

"Excellent!" Rad said, steering High Wire down the mountain path.

As the three friends headed for home, they couldn't help but feel torn between the fact that they had just had the coolest adventure ever and the realization that their planet could soon become the battleground for a four-million-year-old galactic war.

****

The next morning at school, Rad, Carlos, and Alexis greeted each other quietly. They had promised Optimus Prime and each other to keep the events of the previous day a secret. As they walked down the hall toward their first class, Billy and Fred rushed up to the trio.

"So what happened to you guys yesterday?" Billy asked in a knowing way. He didn't want to let on that he and Fred had followed the three friends up the mountain. He also didn't want them to know that he had run at the first sign of trouble.

"Yeah," Fred asked, following Billy's lead as he always did. "Have any great adventures?"

"Not really," Alexis replied with a shrug. "Just a pleasant little ride through the mountains."

Walking quickly past Billy and Fred, with Rad and Carlos on either side of her, Alexis just couldn't resist flashing a smile at her two best friends. The three gently banged their fists together, then headed off to class.

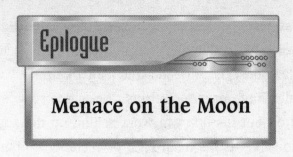

Menace on the Moon

Winds whipped across the barren surface of the moon. Gray clouds billowed around a huge spacecraft sticking out of the powdery lunar soil. A blinding flash momentarily lit the landscape. When the flash faded, Megatron and his army of Decepticons stood assembled before the section of the Mini-cons' ship that had crashed on the moon.

Completing his warp gate transport, Megatron pried open the hatch to the ship, then stepped inside. Having been activated by the green beam from the other section of the Mini-cons' ship on Earth, this part of the ship pulsed with energy. Megatron plugged a connector from his own robotic brain into the ship's main computer. He quickly learned all he needed to know about its power and capabilities.

"This is better than I could have hoped for!" he shouted as control panels flashed to life, and the ship's main systems blinked on after years of inactivity. "This ship will make a fine fortress from which I will lead my assault against the Autobots and planet Earth!"

Bellowing orders to his Decepticon soldiers, Megatron put his army to work setting up the ancient ship to serve as his main base of operations. Stepping back out onto the moon's lifeless surface, Megatron scanned in all directions.

His face broke into a broad, evil smile. His scans revealed that the green Mini-con beam which led him to this ship had also split into many smaller beams, each of which would lead him to another Mini-con somewhere on Earth or the moon.

"So, there are Mini-cons here on the moon, too!" he announced gleefully. "I will get one for myself and some for my fellow Decepticons. That will even things out a bit. Then I will return to Earth and destroy Optimus Prime and the Autobots once and for all! No one and nothing will be able to stop me," Megatron vowed as he gazed menacingly at the Earth.

Will Megatron's evil plan succeed? Find out in the next Transformers chapter book, *Race for the Mini-con Robots*.